THE PILGRIM FATHERS

James told the Puritans, an extra zealous group of Protestants, that if they did not conform to the Church of England they would be 'harried from the land'. A small group of them, unwilling to conform, fled to Holland to escape persecution in 1608 and 12 years later set sail for the new colony of Virginia, in North America. After several false starts, the group of Puritans, known as the Pilgrim Fathers, set sail for America from Plymouth on 16th September 1620 aboard the 'Mayflower'. Life in the new colony was harsh, but they instigated a system of self-government which formed the basis for the American system of government.

PEACE CONFERENCE

The Scots had frequently formed an alliance with Spain against England, their common enemy, and within a year of acceding to the English throne James initiated peace talks with Spain. The talks culminated in a peace conference in 1604, held at Somerset House, in London, between English and Spanish diplomats.

📖 SHAKESPEARE'S SONNETS

William Shakespeare (1564-1616), although better known as a playwright, wrote his plays in iambic pentameter (a form of verse) and also wrote a series of sonnets, or love poems, published in 1609. Sonnets were short, 14-line poems introduced into England from Italy by Sir Thomas Wyatt.

PROTESTANTS COLONISE ULSTER

Following the collapse of the Irish rebellion, led by the Earls of Tyrone and Tyrconnel, Ulster was colonised by English and Scottish Protestants. Although England and Ireland had long been at war, albeit intermittently, it was this act, perhaps more than any other, that led to the religious and political divisions within Ireland, laying the foundations for the modern 'troubles'.

✟ AUTHORISED VERSION OF THE BIBLE

In 1604 James commissioned 54 scholars to write a new translation of the Bible. It was written in everyday English, using a vocabulary of just 5000 words, and published in 1611. For nearly four centuries it has remained the most widely read book in the English language. Ironically, although intended to unite the divided religious beliefs of the nation, by promoting individual conscience and judgement, it led to the development of Puritanism and was instrumental in causing the Civil War of 1642-9.

ANNE OF DENMARK

James married Anne of Denmark in Oslo in 1589 and together they had nine children. The Queen's House, at Greenwich, was begun by him as an out-of-town residence for Anne, but was abandoned on her death. Today, it forms part of the National Maritime Museum complex and contains a fine collection of contemporary paintings and furnishings.

📜 GOVERNMENT   ⚗ HEALTH & MEDICINE   ⚖ JUSTICE   ✟ RELIGION   ✂ SCIENCE

Bates
Robert Winter
Christopher Wright
John Wright
Thomas Percy
Guido (Guy) Fawkes
Robert Catesby
Thomas Winter

THE CONSPIRATORS

Altogether there were 12 conspirators in the plot. They were led by Sir Robert Catesby who, along with others, had already taken part in one ill-fated rebellion when they sided with the Earl of Essex against Elizabeth I. Among the conspirators was a man called John Johnson, who was born a Protestant but later converted to Catholicism. He was an explosives expert who had been fighting in Flanders for the Spanish army and who was given the responsibility of setting the charge beneath Parliament. He afterwards confessed, under torture, to being one Guido (Guy) Fawkes.

THE FAILED ATTEMPT

One of the conspirators, Thomas Percy, had connections at court, which he used to rent a house near the House of Lords where he could store his fuel stocks. From there they dug a tunnel beneath the Parliament building and filled it with barrels of gunpowder. Suspicions had already been aroused prior to the eventual discovery and a 24-hour watch was mounted on the cellar by the conspirators.

BETRAYAL AND CAPTURE

The plotters made a fatal mistake by showing compassion towards fellow Catholics who they knew would be sitting in Parliament on the intended day of the explosion. A secret message was sent to one of the conspirators' brother-in-law, Lord Monteagle, warning him to avoid attending the state opening, but he informed the Privy Council. Lord Suffolk conducted a search of the cellars and uncovered the plot at about midnight on 4th November.

🏛 ARCHITECTURE   📖 ARTS & LITERATURE   ⚑ EXPLORATION   🔥 FAMOUS BATTLES

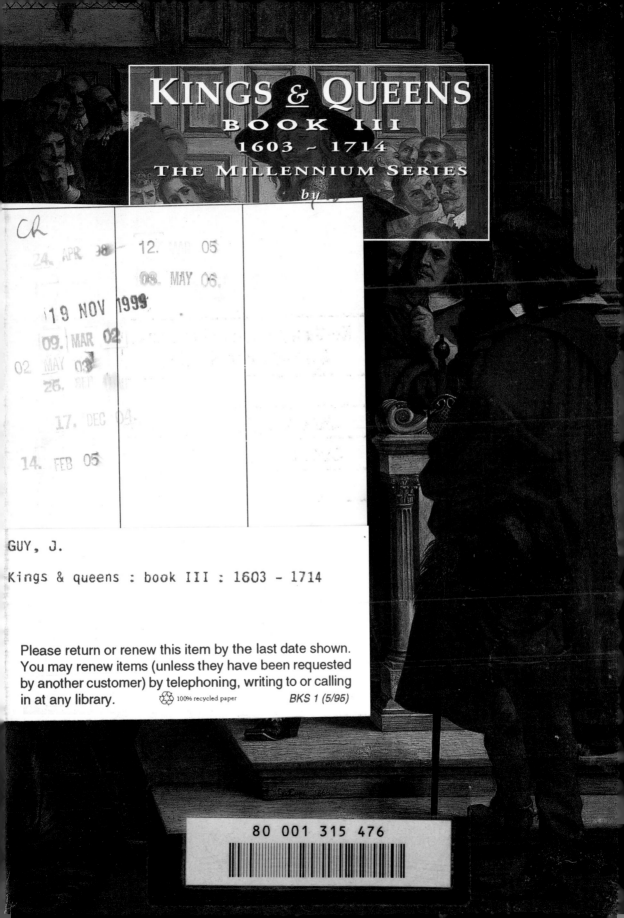

KINGS & QUEENS
BOOK III
1603 ~ 1714
THE MILLENNIUM SERIES

by

JAMES I

BORN 1566 • ACCEDED 1603 • DIED 1625

James's parents were Mary Queen of Scots and Henry Stewart, Lord Darnley. He succeeded to the Scottish throne as James VI when just a few months old. He was Henry VII's great-great-grandson and Elizabeth I's closest relation when she died in 1603. When he was crowned King James I of England he thus united the crowns of Scotland and England. He was, by all accounts, a small, awkward and very ungainly man who had a speech impediment, caused by having a tongue too large for his mouth. His manners and personal hygiene were atrocious. It is claimed he never washed and his skin reputedly felt like black satin.

'THE WISEST FOOL IN CHRISTENDOM'

Although James was a well-educated and learned man, it is difficult to take him seriously as a great monarch. He was something of a scholar and wrote various treatises including one on witchcraft and another on the evils of smoking tobacco, but he seemed unable to focus either his wit or his intelligence. His governance was weak and he relied heavily on his favourites at court, earning him the nickname 'the wisest fool in Christendom', given to him by the Spanish ambassador Count Gondomar.

THE KING'S FAVOURITES

One of the principal reasons for James's unpopularity, both at court and with his people, was his choice of favourite advisers, Robert Kerr, created Earl of Somerset, and George Villiers, who later became Duke of Buckingham. Kerr encouraged James to make peace with the hated Spanish, while Buckingham became so powerful that as the king sank into senility in later life he virtually ruled the country unaided.

DIVINE RIGHT OF KINGS

James had ruled in Scotland as James VI for 36 years under the doctrine of the 'Divine Right of Kings', which held that kings were appointed by God and were beyond judgement from their fellow men. For the English this was an unacceptable form of government. Parliament had long campaigned to reduce the power of the monarchy and when James ruled for long periods without Parliament he became increasingly unpopular. In 1605 an attempt was made to assassinate him.

RALEIGH EXECUTED

Sir Walter Raleigh, who had been one of Elizabeth I's favourites, fell from grace under James I. He was convicted on a trumped-up charge of treason in 1603, but his execution was commuted to imprisonment because of his popularity. Released after 15 years to take part in the ill-fated voyage to discover El Dorado, he was executed in 1618 for attacking the Spanish.

1603 James VI of Scotland is crowned James I of England. **1603** Sir Walter Raleigh arrested	for treason and imprisoned for 15 years. **1604** Somerset House Peace Conference between England and Spain.	**1604** James commissions new English translation of Bible. **1604** Hampton Court Conference	between Anglicans and Puritans. **1605** Gunpowder Plot, attempt by Catholic rebels to blow up Parliament.	**1607** Irish rebellion against English rule put down. **1607** Northern Ireland settled by Protestants

🏛 ARCHITECTURE   📖 ARTS & LITERATURE   🏴 EXPLORATION   💣 FAMOUS BATTLES

THE GUNPOWDER PLOT
1605

lthough perhaps the most remembered and commemorated event in British history, the Gunpowder Plot is shrouded in mystery. As a Protestant, James I was under considerable pressure to strengthen the throne by introducing strict, anti-Catholic laws. The traditional view is that a group of Catholic nobles attempted to assassinate the king and destroy his Protestant Parliament, but many now believe the whole plot was a Protestant contrivance to justify their harsh treatment of the Catholics.

BACKGROUND TO THE PLOT

James I was an unpopular king, particularly with the Catholics, who petitioned him for fairer treatment but were ignored. There had already been several failed attempts to depose him in 1603, after which a plot was devised to blow up the king during the state opening of Parliament in February 1605. Unfortunately, the opening was put back until November, which increased the risk of detection.

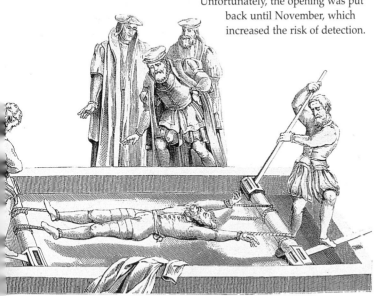

TORTURE

On hearing news that the plot had been discovered, several of the conspirators fled London, only to be later captured by the authorities. Catesby and three others were killed, while the remaining eight were arrested. They were first tortured, then tried and executed by being hanged, drawn and quartered.

BONFIRE NIGHT

The Gunpowder Plot is still commemorated with bonfire celebrations and firework displays every 5th November, the date when Parliament would have been destroyed.

PAGAN OVERTONES

It has often been claimed that the Gunpowder Plot was contrived by the authorities to justify the harsh treatment of Catholics by the Protestant government, but there may also be pagan overtones. Many aspects of the pagan, pre-Christian religion were still widely practised, but 'Christianised' by the church to make them acceptable. All-Hallows Eve was an ancient 'fire festival' when livestock was slaughtered for the onset of winter, at which a sacrifice was originally made. The festival may have been 'Christianised' by shifting the emphasis to celebrating the uncovering of the Gunpowder Plot. It is interesting to note that men called 'guisers' lit the fires at pagan festivals and the conspirator John Johnson only confessed to being 'Guido Fawkes' on being tortured, so the whole thing may have been a contrivance, with the burning of the guy replacing the ritual sacrifice.

🏛 GOVERNMENT   ⚗ HEALTH & MEDICINE   ⚖ JUSTICE   ✝ RELIGION   ⎇ SCIENCE

💣 CIVIL WAR

The arguments that had raged between the monarchy and Parliament for several centuries finally came to a head during the reign of Charles I, when civil war broke out (see pages 8-9) between 1642-49.

⚖️ PETITION OF RIGHT

In 1628 Charles was forced to acknowledge the 'Petition of Right', giving certain rights and liberties to Parliament and challenging royal power. Its four main demands were: taxation should be levied only with parliamentary consent; no-one should be jailed without trial; martial law should be abolished and no troops should be billeted in private households.

📖 VAN DYCK

The painter Anthony Van Dyck was born in the Spanish Netherlands, in what is now Belgium, in 1599. His revolutionary style of portraiture caught the eye of Charles I, who invited him to live in England as the court painter, where he remained until his death in 1641.

GALILEO GALILEI (1564-1642)

Galileo Galilei was born at Pisa, Italy, and became one of the greatest scientists of all time. He developed the use of a pendulum to record time and he perfected a refracting telescope, using it to discover the four moons of Jupiter in 1610. He also discovered that Earth's moon reflects the light of the sun. In later life he was imprisoned for acknowledging Copernicus's theory that the sun, not the Earth, was at the centre of our solar system.

THE LONG AND SHORT PARLIAMENTS

Charles's rule without Parliament became increasingly difficult as time went on. In 1637 he forced the English Prayer Book onto Scotland, which led to open rebellion. Unable to contain the revolt, Charles was forced to recall Parliament three years later. The first attempt was short-lived and lasted only three weeks (known as the 'Short Parliament'). Charles quarrelled with Parliament again, eventually resulting in civil war. Parliament was recalled again, this time lasting until 1660 (known as the 'Long Parliament'). Between 1649-60 England was run by Parliament as a republic.

HENRIETTA MARIA

Charles married Henrietta Maria, daughter of the French king, Henry IV, in 1625 shortly after acceding to the throne. She was only 16 years old and of slightly gawky appearance and the two were not immediately attracted to one another. After 1628 when the king's favourite, the Duke of Buckingham, was assassinated, Charles turned to her for comfort and they became a devoted couple. After Charles's execution in 1649 Henrietta returned to France.

EXECUTION

Charles remains the only British monarch to have been formally charged with treason and executed. Parliament took the unprecedented step of trying the king for waging war against his own people, though Charles refused to acknowledge the legality of the court or to justify his actions. The trial began on 20th January 1649 and lasted just one week. Found guilty, he was executed three days later, on 30th January, by beheading, to a very mixed reaction from the populace.

1625	1627	1629	a Dutch artist, to settle	1640
James's second son succeeds to the throne as Charles I.	*England declares war on France once again.*	*Charles dissolves Parliament again, rules without them until 1640.*	*in England and become court painter.*	*Short Parliament summoned.*
1626	**1628**	**1632**	**1637**	**1640**
Charles dissolves Parliament.	*The Petition of Right is presented to the king.*	*Charles invites Van Dyck,*	*Charles tries to force English prayer book onto Scots.*	*Long Parliament Summoned; lasts until 1660.*

🏛 ARCHITECTURE   📖 ARTS & LITERATURE   ⚑ EXPLORATION   💣 FAMOUS BATTLES

CHARLES I

BORN 1600 • ACCEDED 1625 • EXECUTED 1649

C harles I was another who was not born to be king and did not expect to rule, only inheriting the crown following the death of his elder brother, Henry, in 1612. A slight man of diminutive stature, he also had a slight stammer, reflecting his shyness and lack of self-confidence. He was an intelligent man and a great patron of the arts who carried a dignified air, far removed from the appalling personal manners of his father.

SPECIAL PRIVILEGE

Like his father, James I, Charles believed uncompromisingly in the 'Divine Right of Kings'. Although a medieval doctrine, the power of the monarchy had been considerably reduced in England since those times with the growth in power of Parliament. Not so in Scotland, however, the Stuarts' ancestral homeland, where kings believed they ruled with divine grace and were answerable only to God, not to their fellow men.

CHARLES DISSOLVES PARLIAMENT

Charles's belief in his 'divine' right to rule unhindered frequently brought him into conflict with Parliament. Following the death of his favourite George Villiers, Duke of Buckingham, Charles decided to dissolve Parliament, ruling on his own for 11 years, between 1629-40 using the Court of the Star Chamber and the Court of High Commission to support his actions and dismiss any opposition.

FAMILY MAN

Although a shy man by nature, Charles was very much aware of his responsibilities as king and performed his duties with quiet dignity. He often overcompensated for his shyness, which was seen by many as haughty arrogance. Basically a family man, he was happiest when surrounded by his wife and children (of which he had nine).

1641	1642	War between Charles	1644	him up to Cromwell.
The Court of the Star Chamber abolished.	Charles tries unsuccessfully to arrest five members of Parliament.	and Parliament.	Royalists defeated at Battle of Marston Moor.	1649
		1642		Civil War ends.
1641		Royalists defeat	1646	1649
Catholic revolt in Ireland; many Protestants massacred.	1642	Parliament at Battle of Edgehill.	Charles surrenders to Scots, but they give	Charles arrested, tried and executed.
	Outbreak of Civil			

📜 GOVERNMENT   🥣 HEALTH & MEDICINE   ⚖️ JUSTICE   ✝ RELIGION   🗒 SCIENCE

THE CIVIL WAR
(1642-1649)

Although England had frequently witnessed civil wars, these were mostly local and regional. The Civil War of 1642-49 was the first time the entire country had ranged itself into two distinct factions between king and Parliament, and the first time since the Battle of Bosworth in 1485 that fellow Englishmen had taken up arms against one another. The Stuart notion of ruling by divine right was certain to lead to conflict with Parliament, which came to a head in 1642 when Charles tried to arrest five members of Parliament. The Civil War was a turning point in our constitutional history, for even though the monarchy was restored in 1660 following a brief period as a republic, it was never again able to wield such power and became much more accountable.

PRINCE RUPERT

Prince Rupert was the German-born nephew of Charles I who came to his uncle's aid in 1642 at the age of 23. A talented young man of science, he quickly became also an outstanding military commander. His speciality was lightning cavalry charges, using lightly armed soldiers, who attacked the ill-equipped and inexperienced Parliamentary troops at full gallop, making best use of the element of surprise.

CAVALIERS

The Royalist forces were known as Cavaliers and were usually clothed in resplendent uniforms based on court dress of the day, including knee-length leather boots, tunics and flamboyant hats complete with plumes.

ROUNDHEADS

The Parliamentarians were less well-equipped, especially in the early years of the war. Their uniforms were much simpler and consisted of leather over-tunics, metal helmets and, later, metal breastplates.

ARCHITECTURE   ARTS & LITERATURE   EXPLORATION   FAMOUS BATTLES

DEATH WARRANT

At his trial, Charles refused to acknowledge the court and refused to plead. He wore a black suit and remained eloquent and dignified throughout the proceedings. His death warrant (shown here) was signed by 59 chosen republicans and stated that he should be executed by beheading. When the monarchy was restored in 1660 most of the signatories fled abroad, or escaped execution themselves by repenting their actions, but 10 of the regicides who refused to repent were executed for treason.

NEW MODEL ARMY

In February 1645 Parliament created a revolutionary new military system, the New Model Army. Nationally organised and regularly paid, it was the basis of the armed services today. Commanding officers were promoted to rank based on their abilities rather than on their social standing. Sir Thomas Fairfax was commander of the new army, with Oliver Cromwell, a leading figure in the Parliamentary cause, the Lieutenant-General. Well drilled and disciplined, Cromwell personally oversaw the army's rigorous training programme.

A PRISONER IN CARISBROOKE CASTLE

In 1646 Charles surrendered to the Scots, expecting compassion, but they handed him over to Cromwell. He escaped, briefly, but was recaptured and imprisoned in Carisbrooke Castle, on the Isle of Wight, where he remained for a year.

◗※ BATTLE OF EDGEHILL

The Battle of Edgehill was the first major conflict of the Civil War. Fought on a hill in the Cotswolds, both sides were evenly matched, consisting of about 12,000 men each, and both lost about 2,500 by the end of the day, over half through desertion. It was not a pitched battle and both sides seemed reluctant to fight their fellow Englishmen, but it marked the beginning of seven years of bloody conflict. Both sides claimed victory, but the Royalist forces had the better of the day, though they failed to capitalize on their advantage.

◗※ BATTLE OF MARSTON MOOR

The early years of the war belonged to the Royalists, who at one stage looked like winning, under the daring leadership of Prince Rupert. The turning point came in 1644, at the Battle of Marston Moor. Cromwell won a resounding victory, earning Rupert's respect in his epitaph when he called the Parliamentarians 'ironsides'.

◗※ BATTLE OF NASEBY

Cromwell's New Model Army was put to the test at the Battle of Naseby in June 1645. The Parliamentary army, at 15,000 strong, was twice the size of the Royalist force and easily won the day. One of the most decisive victories of the campaign, it effectively marked the end of the Civil War. Charles was captured and imprisoned the following year and although the war dragged on until 1649, the Royalists were a spent force after the battle.

THE COMMONWEALTH
(1649-1660)

ritain's only brush with republicanism was short-lived. The dominant figure throughout the Civil War, and later the Commonwealth, was Oliver Cromwell (see pages 12-13) and, although he devised a new, and in many ways fairer system of government, it was never fully democratic and it disintegrated when he died. Although a brilliant leader, the strength of his leadership lay in his personal qualities and not in the reforms he introduced. His successor, his son Richard, proved an inept politician and within two years of Oliver Cromwell's death, Parliament recalled the monarchy.

CHARLES II GOES INTO EXILE

·Following the defeat of the Scots at the Battle of Dunbar, (see bottom right) Charles II led another rebellious Scottish force against Cromwell at the Battle of Worcester in 1651, but he was defeated and afterwards forced into exile, first to France and then to Holland.

THE DUTCH WARS

As a direct result of the commercial rivalry caused by the Navigation Act, the first of a series of three wars between England and Holland broke out between 1652-4. England's military and naval prowess increased significantly in the early years of the Commonwealth under Cromwell's leadership and the Dutch fleet was routed by Robert Blake.

THE RUMP PARLIAMENT

The 'Rump Parliament' was a derisive name given to the 'Long Parliament'. It had sat for 13 years and many of its members had deserted leaving, by 1653, fewer than 60 of its original 490 members. During the Civil War it was Cromwell's army that had won the day, not Parliament, which in his eyes seemed as corrupt as the monarchy itself. In 1653 he dismissed the Rump Parliament and ruled instead with the army.

1649	*declared a republic.*	**1650**	**1651**	*protect English shipping.*
Council of State appoints	**1649**	*Scots royalists*	*Charles II claims the throne,*	**1653**
Oliver Cromwell as	*Irish rebels, loyal*	*defeated at Battle*	*but is defeated by Cromwell at*	*Rump Parliament*
Chairman to rule country.	*to Charles, defeated*	*of Dunbar.*	*Worcester and forced into exile.*	*dismissed by Cromwell.*
1649	*at Battles of Wexford*	**1650**	**1651**	**1653**
England is	*and Drogheda.*	*Vacuum pump invented.*	*Navigation Act passed to*	*Cromwell declared Lord*

🏛 ARCHITECTURE   📖 ARTS & LITERATURE   ↳ EXPLORATION   💣 FAMOUS BATTLES

ENGLAND DECLARED A REPUBLIC

The period known as the Commonwealth can roughly be divided into two phases. The first, known as the Republic, spanned the period 1649-53, where Cromwell attempted to govern within the existing parliamentary structure, but drastic reforms were needed if the monarchy were to be replaced with a sustainable form of government. The second period was known as the Protectorate (see below).

THE PROTECTORATE

The second period of the Commonwealth was known as the Protectorate and lasted from 1653-9. When Cromwell dismissed the Long Parliament in 1653 he effectively set himself up as leader of a dictatorship, assuming the title Lord Protector of England. He ruled with the aid of his New Model Army and formed a new Parliament which, in 1657, offered him the monarchy, but he refused. In all, three Protectorate Parliaments were called by Cromwell, and each was dismissed by him as it failed to live up to his ideals. When Cromwell died in 1658 his son Richard became Lord Protector, but he lacked his father's qualities and was dismissed by Parliament in 1660 when they invited Charles II to return as king.

COUNCIL OF STATE

The remaining members of the Long Parliament, who had called for Charles I's execution, formed a Council of State in 1649 with Oliver Cromwell as chairman. Many of the members were interested only in their own needs and obstructed many of Cromwell's parliamentary reforms, which prompted Cromwell to rule as dictator.

☀ SIEGE OF DROGHEDA

Irish and Scots royalists led a combined rebellion against Parliament following Charles I's execution, though in the case of the Irish this was seen more as a means of removing English rule from Ireland than in supporting Charles II's cause. Cromwell defeated the Irish at Wexford and at the Siege of Drogheda in 1649.

🗒 NAVIGATION ACT

In 1651 the Navigation Act was passed, which gave English merchant ships a monopoly over foreign imports and exports from English ports. This had the effect of bolstering the English economy and led directly to conflict with Holland.

☀ BATTLE OF DUNBAR

Following the execution of Charles I his son, Charles II, was proclaimed king by the Scots, despite their having betrayed his father by handing him over to Parliament. Cromwell's answer was swift and decisive. He defeated the Scots at the Battle of Dunbar in 1650.

Protector of England.	*Parliament and rules with*	**1657**	*by Cromwell.*	*Lord Protector.*
1654	*his army, headed by 11*	*Cromwell offered the*	**1658**	**1660**
First Protectorate	*Major-Generals.*	*throne, but refuses.*	*Oliver Cromwell dies.*	*Restoration of*
Parliament called.	**1655**	**1658**	**1658**	*the monarchy*
1655	*English take Jamaica*	*Third Protectorate*	*Oliver's son, Richard*	*recommended by the*
Cromwell dismisses	*from the Spanish.*	*Parliament dismissed*	*Cromwell, becomes*	*new Parliament.*

📜 GOVERNMENT   ⚗ HEALTH & MEDICINE   ⚖ JUSTICE   ✝ RELIGION   🗒 SCIENCE

OFFERED THE CROWN

Cromwell was offered the crown of England by the Protectorate Parliament in 1657. His attempts to reform government failed and he had to rely more and more on military force, which caused further divisions. By inviting him to become king, Parliament thought the divided country might unite behind a common cause, but Cromwell refused, saying that he was against the principle of hereditary rule. His own generals were against the idea also and threatened revolt if he accepted the crown.

OLIVER CROMWELL
(Lord Protector)
BORN 1599 • APPOINTED CHAIRMAN OF COUNCIL OF STATE 1649
APPOINTED LORD PROTECTOR 1653 • DIED 1658

Oliver Cromwell was born in 1599, the son of a wealthy Huntingdonshire squire. He was tall, though not handsome, and of somewhat slovenly appearance. He entered politics at the age of 29 but had a remarkably uneventful career until the outbreak of the Civil War. A self-taught soldier who learned his tactical skills by reading military accounts, he led a cavalry unit in East Anglia at the outset of the war. He was a charismatic man who quickly rose through the ranks by showing his military prowess and by 1644 he was appointed Lieutenant-General for all the Parliamentary armies and came to be regarded as one of the finest commanders in Europe.

JAMAICA CAPTURED

While many of his fellow countrymen viewed Cromwell with suspicion and even hatred because of the harsh laws he imposed, those abroad regarded him with grudging respect and admiration. His reorganisation of the armed services gave him great prestige in Europe. The Dutch were routed at sea and many of the Spanish dominions were attacked, including Jamaica, which was taken in 1655.

ARCHITECTURE   ARTS & LITERATURE   EXPLORATION   FAMOUS BATTLES

LORD PROTECTOR OF ENGLAND

When he realised that Parliament did not entirely support his reforms, Cromwell decided to go it alone and in 1653 declared himself Lord Protector of England. Despite his democratic and religious ideals, he never sought open and free elections for fear of losing, because many of his policies were unpopular. Instead, he justified his dictatorial stance by claiming that he acted in the name of God for the people's best interests; ironically, not too dissimilar to the Stuart-held belief of the 'Divine Right of Kings'!

DEVOUTLY RELIGIOUS

Cromwell was a devoutly religious man, tolerant of most religious views (except Catholicism) and adopted a Puritan lifestyle although, contrary to popular view, his own beliefs were not extreme and he was not averse to pleasure seeking, in moderation. He believed passionately in his mission to remove the tyrant monarchy from Britain and replace it with a fairer system of government and felt that in so doing he was being guided by God's hand.

RESTORATION OF THE MONARCHY

The act of removing what he saw as a tyrannical monarchy proved an easier task than finding a suitable system of government to replace it. Cromwell had largely won the Civil War with his New Model Army, with little assistance from Parliament, and when he later came to introduce radical reforms he discovered that Parliament was just as corrupt as the monarchy had ever been. Consequently, he introduced stricter and stricter methods to control the country which had the effect of stifling the population and turned many people against the idea of a republic. Within two years of his death, Parliament itself invited Charles II to return from exile as king. Certain conditions were imposed on his restoration to prevent royal excesses occurring again, but by and large the return of the monarchy was welcomed.

PURITAN LIFESTYLE

Cromwell had a vision to reform corruption in society, not just in removing a self-indulgent monarchy, but in restoring the people to a more righteous way of life. He followed a Puritan lifestyle and rejected many of the old religious ways, which he saw as popish. Festivals such as Christmas and May Day were abolished, drinking and swearing were forbidden, as was profaning the Sabbath, and everyone was required to attend church. He was not averse to enjoyment, but its excesses were strictly controlled, making him very unpopular with the people.

📖 JOHN MILTON

John Milton, born in 1608, represented the spirit of the age in his deeply religious poetry. A devout Puritan, he became the Commonwealth's semi-official spokesman in 1649 but, like Cromwell himself, he saw all his dreams and ideals shattered in his lifetime. The so-called 'English Revolution' had come to nothing. His most famous works, 'Paradise Lost' and 'Paradise Regained', express his disillusionment with the politics of the day. He went blind at the age of 44 and died in 1674.

🏛 GOVERNMENT   ⚕ HEALTH & MEDICINE   ⚖ JUSTICE   ✝ RELIGION   🔬 SCIENCE

CHARLES II

BORN 1630 • ACCEDED 1660 • DIED 1685

*f*ollowing the execution of his father, Charles I, in 1649 and his unsuccessful attempts to ascend the throne, Charles was forced into exile, initially to France, but afterwards to Germany and Holland. Although technically still king, Charles had little money and for 11 years lived a frugal existence. When Oliver Cromwell died in 1658 the Commonwealth began to collapse. To avert another civil war, Parliament asked the exiled king to return to England. He arrived in London on 29th May 1660, on his 30th birthday. Cromwell's body was exhumed and hanged at Tyburn, but otherwise the Restoration passed without further recriminations.

CHARLES II

The restoration of Charles II was greeted with wild enthusiasm by a population that had suffered considerable repression under Puritan rule. Although Charles acknowledged having 14 illegitimate children, he had none by his wife. On his death the throne passed to his brother, James.

FLIGHT FOR FREEDOM

After the execution of his father, Charles led a revolt against Parliament. He lost to Cromwell at the Battle of Worcester in 1651 and fled to France.

THE NAVAL COLLEGE

The royal palace of Placentia, that formerly stood at Greenwich, was rebuilt by Charles II to designs by Sir Christopher Wren. The magnificent buildings were later converted for use as a naval hospital, college and maritime museum.

1660 Charles II asked to return to England as king.	**1661** First Parliament of Charles's reign called.	*from holding governmental posts.* **1662** Act of Uniformity makes Puritans accept Anglican Church.	**1662** Royal Society given royal charter. **1665/7** War breaks out with Holland, leads to	*humiliating naval defeat for English at Chatham.* **1665** Extensive outbreak of the plague, especially in London.
1660 Samuel Pepys begins writing his diaries.	**1661** Corporation Act prevents Nonconformists			

🏛 ARCHITECTURE   📖 ARTS & LITERATURE   ⮒ EXPLORATION   ⚫ FAMOUS BATTLES

✝ A CHANGE OF MIND

Charles II was a flamboyant character who resented the stifling attitudes of the church, particularly after the puritanical zeal of Oliver Cromwell's time. On his deathbed in 1685 he reverted to Catholicism.

⎍ THE ROYAL SOCIETY

From 1645 a group of people, interested in scientific discovery, began meeting on a regular basis in Oxford and London. Charles was himself very interested in science and in 1662 granted them a charter, marking the founding of the Royal Society.

▤ THE 'WHIGS' & 'TORIES'

The names of the political parties Whigs (Liberals) and Tories (Conservatives) have their origins in the Civil War. The Whigs, founded by Lord Shaftesbury, were pro-Parliament, while the Tories supported the monarchy. The names were first used in 1679.

THE DUTCH WARS

There were three separate wars with Holland during the 17th century, one during the Commonwealth and two during Charles's reign. In 1667 the English suffered a humiliating defeat when the Dutch sailed up the River Medway and laid waste the fleet anchored at Chatham Dockyard, in Kent.

A MERRY MONARCH

When in 1660 Charles was invited to become king, as part of the bargain he had to marry Catherine of Braganza, from Portugal. It was a loveless marriage and Charles, who was tall and handsome, took an estimated 17 mistresses. The most notable of these was Nell Gwynne, whom he openly courted and who is believed to have given him two sons. Charles was a popular figure who delighted in pleasurable pursuits, such as gambling, hunting and boating.

SIR CHRISTOPHER WREN

Sir Christopher Wren was born in 1632 and by the age of 29 was already Professor of Astronomy at Oxford. He was a founder member of the Royal Society and was interested in all aspects of science. He came late to architecture, when he was asked to design the Sheldonian Theatre at Oxford. He went on to design many churches and public buildings in the Classical style. In 1666 he submitted a plan to build a dome for the medieval St. Paul's Cathedral, London. When the cathedral burned down in the Great Fire, he was asked to design a replacement cathedral. The result was the magnificent cathedral we see today. Begun in 1675 it was completed in 1710. Wren died in 1723 aged 91.

1666	**1670**	*founded for fur trading*	**1678**	*attempt to*
Great Fire of London	*Charles signs Treaty of Dover*	*in North America.*	*The Popish Plot,*	*assassinate Charles.*
breaks out.	*and agrees in secret to restore*	**1673**	*supposedly a Catholic plot*	**1685**
1666	*Catholicism to England.*	*Test Act prevents*	*to assassinate the king.*	*Charles converts*
Isaac Newton discovers	**1670**	*Catholics from holding*	**1683**	*to Catholicism on*
the solar spectrum.	*Hudson Bay Company*	*government office.*	*Rye House Plot; a further*	*his deathbed.*

▤ GOVERNMENT   ⚕ HEALTH & MEDICINE   ⚖ JUSTICE   ✝ RELIGION   ⎍ SCIENCE

HOW THE FIRE STARTED

The fire started in the premises of Thomas Farriner, in Pudding Lane, at about midnight on Saturday 1st September 1666. Farriner was a baker and, according to a statement he gave later, he checked his ovens before retiring to bed. He was awakened a few hours later by smoke and fled to nearby premises. His own housemaid was the fire's first victim. Several nearby warehouses containing pitch aided the spread of the fire, assisted by a fanning wind. The site of the fire is marked by a monument in Pudding Lane, designed by Sir Christopher Wren.

FIGHTING THE FIRE

Defences against the fire were woefully inadequate and consisted principally of leather buckets and hand-squirts (a kind of syphon) with people forming human bucket chains. With no running water supplies, water had to be fetched from the river or from wells. There was no organised fire service and the only effective remedy was to destroy houses in the path of the fire to create fire-breaks. The fire eventually burned itself out on 6th September when the wind changed direction.

THE DAMAGE CAUSED

Many of the buildings of London were constructed of timber and thatch and the fire quickly spread out of control through the narrow streets. It burned for nearly five days, destroying old St. Paul's Cathedral, 88 churches and about 13,200 houses and other buildings in its wake, making an estimated 100,000 people homeless, though miraculously only nine people died.

EXTENT OF THE BLAZE

The map on the left shows the extent of the blaze. Over four-fifths of the City of London, within the old city walls, was destroyed, covering an area in excess of 430 acres.

Afbeelding van de **STADT LONDON.**
Aenwijsende hoe verre de selve verbrandt is, en wat plaetsen noch ongeschreven zijn.

Representation curieuse de l'embrasement de la **VILLE de LONDRES.**
Avec une Demonstration exacte de ce qui en est denué, de ville.

Delineation of the **CITIE LONDON.**
Shewing how far the said citie is burnt down, and what places they yet remain standing.

🏛 ARCHITECTURE   📖 ARTS & LITERATURE   ⚑ EXPLORATION   💣 FAMOUS BATTLES

FIRE & PLAGUE

(1665-66)

etween June 1665 and September 1666 London suffered two quite catastrophic disasters. The first of these was a serious outbreak of the plague followed, a year later, by the most devastating fire this country has ever witnessed. Many Puritans saw it as divine retribution following the Restoration of the monarchy. Ironically, although the outbreak of plague continued a while longer, the fire stemmed the worst of its ravages. Although localised outbreaks occurred at intervals for the next two centuries, this was the last major epidemic of plague in England.

OUTBREAK OF PLAGUE

The plague first appeared in Britain in the mid-14th century (though similar diseases may have been around since Saxon times), brought here from the Middle East by flea-infected rats aboard merchant ships. During that outbreak it is estimated between $\frac{1}{3}$ and $\frac{1}{5}$ of the population died. It was principally a disease of the poor, spread by rats in the insanitary living conditions of the time, but no-one was immune. The outbreak of 1665-6, known as the Great Plague, was one of many epidemics that occurred periodically in Britain from the 14th to the 19th centuries and ranks as one of the worst, killing an estimated 100,000 people in London alone. It was more prevalent in towns and many of the rich, including Charles II, moved to country retreats until the epidemic subsided.

REBUILDING LONDON

Charles II himself, and his brother James, are said to have assisted in fighting the fire and the king rode amongst the homeless a few days later to quash rumours that the fire had been started deliberately by England's enemies. Charles saw the opportunity of rebuilding the centre of London to a grand new design and commissioned Christopher Wren to design a new capital. The plans he submitted were never fully carried out, but he was responsible for many new buildings, including a new St. Paul's Cathedral and over 50 other churches.

WHAT IS THE PLAGUE?

The plague is a severe infectious fever caused by the bacterium 'Pasteurella pestis' and is transmitted to man, from rats, by their fleas. There are two forms, bubonic and pneumonic plague. The symptoms of bubonic plague are fever, followed by swollen lymph nodes in the neck, armpits and groin. Dark blotches, caused by internal bleeding, are one reason for its other name, the 'Black Death'. Over half of all victims in the 17th century died within five days. The more serious pneumonic plague infected the lungs and was usually 100% fatal. Although rare, the plague still exists in certain hot countries, but can normally be cured with strong antibiotics.

EFFECTS OF THE PLAGUE

Scarcely a family in the land was unaffected by the plague. One of the principal effects of the disease was the obvious decimation of the population but ironically, for those who survived, living conditions temporarily improved.

Because of the scarcity of labour, particularly after the major epidemics, those who survived were able to command higher wages, until the authorities legislated against it.

🏛 GOVERNMENT   ☕ HEALTH & MEDICINE   ⚖ JUSTICE   ✝ RELIGION   𝄢 SCIENCE

☀ BATTLE OF SEDGMOOR

The Battle of Sedgmoor, fought on 6th July 1685, was the last land battle to be fought in England. It was fought between the Duke of Monmouth who, as Charles II's illegitimate son, claimed the throne, and James II's army. The battle was short-lived and lasted only about four hours. Monmouth's men were hopelessly outnumbered and outmanoeuvred and the royal troops easily won the day.

✝ DECLARATION OF INDULGENCE

James openly encouraged the re-introduction of Catholic rites and institutions in religious and court life, replacing many Protestant government officers with Catholic favourites. In 1688 he introduced the Declaration of Indulgence, which suspended all laws against Catholics and Non-Conformists.

✝ RESTORATION OF CATHOLICISM

James converted to Catholicism in the 1660s, much to the disapproval of Parliament, who removed him from high office and tried, unsuccessfully, to prevent his succession to the throne. He declared from the outset that he intended to restore Catholicism as the main religion of Britain. To help him achieve this he increased the standing army from 6,000 to 30,000, replacing many of the Protestant officers with Catholics.

∂ SIR ISAAC NEWTON

The Stuart age was a period of great advances in science. One of the greatest scientists of the day was Sir Isaac Newton (1642-1727) who made a major contribution to our understanding of mathematics and physics, including the law of gravity. He also developed the reflecting telescope.

Elizabeth Gaunt was burnt for harbouring rebels after the battle of Sedgmoor.

'THE GLORIOUS REVOLUTION'

In 1688 Parliament invited William of Orange, ruler of Holland and James's son-in-law, to restore liberties to England. He landed at Brixham, in Devon, on 5th November 1688, with an invasion force. Although William was not a popular figure, James II had little support himself and the Dutchman was able to march on London and force the king's deposition in a virtually bloodless coup.

DUKE OF MONMOUTH

James, Duke of Monmouth, was the illegitimate son of Charles II and within a few months of James II's accession he led a Protestant rebellion against the Catholic king in a bid for the throne. He was a vain, ambitious man who was used by the king's political adversaries in an attempt to remove him from the throne. The plan was ill-conceived and badly executed, however, resulting in Monmouth's defeat at the Battle of Sedgmoor in Somerset in 1685 and his execution shortly after.

HUGUENOT REFUGEES

In 1682, in France, over 60,000 Protestants had been forcibly converted to Catholicism followed, in 1685, by the revocation of the Edict of Nantes, which no longer made it possible for Protestants (known in France as Huguenots) to practise their religion freely. Many Huguenot refugees fled France and settled in England, particularly on the east coast, bringing their crafts and skills with them. They were especially adept in the art of clothmaking and greatly influenced the trade in this country.

1685	Charles II, leads rebellion	1685	standing army of over	1686
Charles's brother succeeds to the throne as James II.	against James.	Edict of Nantes is revoked in France; many Huguenot	12,000 to intimidate the inhabitants of London.	Dominion of New England established.
1685	1685	refugees flee to England.	1686	1687
Duke of Monmouth the illegitimate son of	Duke of Monmouth defeated at Battle of Sedgmoor, later executed.	1686 James sets up a	James attempts to restore Catholicism to England.	Isaac Newton publishes his first major work

🏛 ARCHITECTURE   📖 ARTS & LITERATURE   ⚑ EXPLORATION   ☀ FAMOUS BATTLES

JAMES II

BORN 1633 • ACCEDED 1685 • DEPOSED 1688 • DIED 1701

*L*ike all the Stuarts, James was a proud, haughty man, who believed strongly in the doctrine of the Divine Right of Kings. He was the second son of Charles I and acceded on the death of his brother, Charles II, who had no legitimate children to inherit the throne. He spent much of his early life in government office and was made Lord High Admiral, serving in the Dutch wars, but aroused considerable opposition from Parliament because of his strong Catholic views. Although tall, handsome and by all accounts well-mannered, because of his arrogance he never won the popular support of his people.

JAMES ABDICATES

When faced with the choice of accepting Parliament's demands or deposition, James refused to compromise his ideals and chose abdication. He was deposed on 23rd December 1688 and forced into exile in France, where he died in 1701, it is believed from syphilis.

TRIAL OF THE SEVEN BISHOPS

As part of his drive towards Catholicism, James ordered all Protestant clergy to read the Declaration of Indulgence out loud in their churches. There was much opposition and many refused. Sancroft, Archbishop of Canterbury, and six other bishops petitioned James to withdraw the order but he had them arrested for seditious libel. They were sent for trial at Westminster, but were acquitted, amidst much jubilation.

JUDGE JEFFREYS & THE BLOODY ASSIZES

Following the Duke of Monmouth's ill-fated attempt to seize the crown, the remaining rebels were put on trial by the notorious Judge Jeffreys. At 40 Jeffreys became the youngest Lord Chancellor and he soon acquired a reputation as being the most brutal. The series of trials against the rebels soon degenerated into a farce as Jeffreys bullied and intimidated the witnesses. He executed over 300 of the Protestant rebels and transported about 1,000 more to the colonies. The infamous trials came to be known as the 'Bloody Assizes'.

on mathematics.
1688
Declaration of Indulgence repeals all anti-Catholic and anti-Non-Conformist laws.

1688
James's second wife, Mary of Modena, gives birth to a son, James Edward, who becomes his favoured Catholic heir.

1688
Trial of the Seven Bishops for seditious libel.
1688
William of Orange, the Dutch ruler, is

invited to accept the throne of England.
1688
The Glorious Revolution; William lands in England and seizes

the throne, virtually unopposed.
1688
James is forced to abdicate and flee to France in exile.

GOVERNMENT   HEALTH & MEDICINE   JUSTICE   RELIGION   SCIENCE

HOW WE GOT OUR PARLIAMENT

MAGNA CARTA

The first milestone in British constitutional history was when the barons forced King John to sign the Magna Carta (or Great Charter) in 1215. The original version contained 63 clauses that curbed absolute royal power. Although largely ignored by subsequent monarchs, it formed the corner-stone of the governmental reforms that followed in later centuries.

SIMON DE MONTFORT

Known as the 'Father of English Parliament', Simon de Montfort determined to make government less exclusive and more accountable by reducing the power of the monarchy. He called the first open English Parliament in 1265, but met his death at the hands of the King's Court (as shown here).

Today we live in a democracy (from the Greek words 'demos', meaning people, and 'kratos', meaning power), governed by an elected body of representatives known as Members of Parliament. We pride ourselves in Britain in having one of the fairest systems of government in the world, but things were not always so. The change from an absolute monarchy to a constitutional monarchy, where the king or queen is merely a figurehead, was a slow process. The Parliament we have today is the result of many centuries of struggle by right-minded people who felt we should all have a say in how our country is governed and many lost their lives in the process.

THE SAXON WITAN

Saxon kings ruled with a council of personally selected advisers known as the Witan, who made all the national decisions. Beneath that were three separate tiers of local government, roughly corresponding to the shire (or county), town and parish councils still in existence today, known as moot councils, though few elements of society were eligible to sit on the councils.

THE FEUDAL SYSTEM

In many respects the Saxon system of government was fairer than the feudal system that followed it. Introduced by the Normans after the Conquest of 1066 the king ruled with absolute power. The moot councils were retained, but they merely acted as the king's agents. Under the feudal system, all land ultimately belonged to the crown, which was then let to various levels of sub-tenants in return for military service.

EDWARD I'S MODEL PARLIAMENT

Edward I agreed, in principle, with Simon de Montfort's call for government reforms. In 1295 he called the first democratically elected (at least partially) Parliament known as the 'Model Parliament', comprising lords, clergy, knights and elected representatives from the community, sitting in two houses, the Lords and the Commons.

🏛 ARCHITECTURE   📖 ARTS & LITERATURE   ⚐ EXPLORATION   ⬥ FAMOUS BATTLES

REFORM ACT OF 1832

Prior to 1832 only certain classes of people were allowed to vote, namely property owners and landowners. The first Reform Act of that year greatly extended the vote and ensured a fairer distribution of parliamentary seats based on population. Subsequent acts in 1867 and 1884 further reformed the system.

SECRET BALLOT

In 1872 the Secret Ballot was introduced into the electoral system to eliminate vote rigging and possible recriminations. Surprisingly, the vote was not extended to all women of 21 and over until 1928.

PARTY POLITICS

The ongoing feud between king and Parliament finally came to a head in the Civil War of 1642-49 (Charles is shown, attempting to arrest 5 members of the Houses of Parliament). Until then, although the monarchy ruled with Parliament, the king could still call or dismiss a parliament at will. The beginnings of the party system of politics emerged at this time.

THE COMMONWEALTH

The Commonwealth (1649-60) was the only period in our history when Parliament ruled as a republic, without a monarchy (see pages 10-11).

BILL OF RIGHTS

Introduced in 1689, the Bill of Rights is usually seen as the second most important constitutional reform after Magna Carta. Its main clauses were that no Catholic could become the ruling monarch and taxes and laws could only be implemented with parliamentary consent.

THE PEOPLE'S CHARTER

In 1838 the People's Charter was issued by a group of people, known as the Chartists, campaigning for political reform. Its main clauses called for the right to vote for everyone, the right for anyone to seek election, secret ballots and equal representation. Although not fully realised until as late as 1944, the Charter forms the basis of our modern constitution.

THE HOUSES OF PARLIAMENT

The present Houses of Parliament were completed in 1867 to designs by Pugin and Barry after the old Palace of Westminster burned down in 1834. Formerly, Parliament met in St. Stephen's Chapel (known as Parliament House), given to the Commons by Edward VI and once part of the royal palace.

GOVERNMENT   HEALTH & MEDICINE   JUSTICE   RELIGION   SCIENCE

💣 SIEGE OF LONDONDERRY

Following James II's deposition in 1688 a Catholic rebellion broke out in an attempt to reinstate him on the throne. The following year the rebels landed in Ireland and laid siege to Londonderry, occupied by Protestant forces loyal to William III, who took cover within the city walls for 105 days before English forces put down the rebellion.

💣 BATTLE OF THE BOYNE

After the failure of his army to take Londonderry, James II travelled south to Drogheda, to the area around the River Boyne. His forces again engaged William III's army (in July 1690) and again faced defeat. This time, however, James gave up the fight and fled to France in exile, where he remained until his death in 1701.

📜 ACT OF UNION

The Act of Union between Britain and Ireland was passed in 1800, but government was still heavily biased in favour of the Protestants even though they were a minority. The movement for Irish Home Rule began to gather momentum, but two Bills (in 1886 and again in 1893) failed to become law. Subsequent English governments failed to resolve the problems in Ireland and in 1920 Ireland was partitioned. The Free State, known as Eire, became a self-governing republic and the six counties of Northern Ireland remained part of the United Kingdom, sharing the same constitutional monarchy as England, Wales and Scotland.

THE NORMANS

The English invasion of Ireland began in 1154-5 during the reign of Henry II. The church in Ireland, though Christian, refused to follow the doctrines of Rome so Pope Adrian IV gave authority to Henry to invade Ireland, annexe the country to England and bring the church into line with Rome. It was not until 1166, however, that Henry sent his first invasion force to Ireland, during a dispute between the Irish kings when one, Dermot MacMurrough, King of Leinster, asked the English king for help. In 1171 Henry himself headed an invasion force. The heavily armoured Normans quickly gained control and he declared himself Lord of Ireland. Later the same year he forced the Irish clergy to acknowledge the pope's authority.

IRELAND DIVIDED

Although there were long-standing divisions in Ireland for many centuries before England's intervention between the various tribes and kingdoms, the religious divisions between Catholic and Protestant, which have become so much a part of the 'troubles' in Ireland in recent years, stem directly from the Tudor period. It was at that time that the first Protestant settlers (known as 'planters') were encouraged to settle in Ireland to strengthen the English position against possible alliances between Ireland, Spain and France. Intermarriage between the settlers and the Irish people, coupled with the growth of Protestantism in general, have subsequently led to deep social divisions between the people of Ireland.

🏛 ARCHITECTURE   📖 ARTS & LITERATURE   ⚑ EXPLORATION   💣 FAMOUS BATTLES

THE MONARCHY OF IRELAND

The story of the Irish monarchy is complex because, like its neighbours, England, Scotland and Wales, it was not unified as a single nation until quite late in its history. The situation was further complicated in Ireland, however, because of interference from England, which sought to annexe it and protect itself from attack. The result was that before Ireland could be properly unified under one king, English kings claimed sovereignty from the 12th century onwards, a situation that perhaps goes some way to explain the deep-rooted divisions within Ireland today.

EARLY IRISH KINGS

Ireland, like Wales, Scotland and ancient Britain, has a Celtic ancestry but, unlike them, was little influenced by Saxon raids (though it was subjected to Danish invasions in the 9th and 10th centuries). Traditionally, six kings ruled separate provinces of Ireland who each swore loyalty to a High King. Each of the kingdoms was further sub-divided into tribes, each with their own leader, also known as kings. The last High King of Ireland was Brian Boru (above), King of Munster, who died in 1014 whilst defending Ireland against the Danes. When he died the remaining kings of the provinces fought an ongoing and, ultimately, unresolved civil war to gain supremacy.

THE TUDORS

Although subsequent medieval monarchs retained an influence over Irish affairs, the country was never fully conquered and several of the Celtic Irish kings continued to rule in defiance of English authority. Many of the English and Norman barons sent to Ireland married Irish women and adopted Irish lifestyles. It was not until the Tudor period that the re-invasion of Ireland became a priority once more. To protect himself from an Irish alliance with France, Henry VIII put down several rebellions against English rule and declared himself king of Ireland in 1541. Elizabeth I (and several of the Stuart kings who followed her) later encouraged Protestant settlements in Ireland to strengthen the English position by granting Irish estates to English nobles.

'THE PALE'

Despite Henry VIII's grandiose claim to be king of Ireland and the subsequent settlements by Protestants under later monarchs (mostly in Ulster) the English never really had much more than a toe-hold in Ireland. Prior to Henry VIII's time, most of the English settlements were confined to Dublin and its surrounding area. It became known as 'the Pale' because of the earth and timber defence works erected around the settlements to ward off attacks by Irish clansmen.

WILLIAM OF ORANGE

In 1688 the English Parliament invited the Protestant Dutch ruler, William of Orange (the name of the Dutch royal house), to depose the Catholic king of England, James II, and rule in his place. He became William III and ruled with Mary II, James's daughter. Not everyone accepted him at first and many Catholics joined James II in his attempt to win back the crown. In Ireland, the Protestants sided with William, while the Catholics supported James.

📕 GOVERNMENT   ⚗ HEALTH & MEDICINE   ⚖ JUSTICE   ✝ RELIGION   🛢 SCIENCE

WILLIAM III & MARY II

WILLIAM III BORN 1650 • ACCEDED 1689 • DIED 1702
MARY II BORN 1662 • ACCEDED 1689 • DIED 1694

*U*ntil 1688 the Protestant Mary was heir to the throne, but when James II's second wife, Mary of Modena, gave birth to a son in that year, succession passed to him. Mary, among many others, doubted the legitimacy of this baby, whom James declared would be brought up a Catholic, which was against Parliament's wishes and prompted the king's deposition later the same year. In 1677 Mary married William of Orange (the name given to the Dutch royal family) who was the son of William of Nassau and Mary Stuart. William was a man of slight build and was never very popular with the English, unlike Mary, who was much liked. She died at the premature age of 32, from smallpox.

INVITATION TO THE ENGLISH THRONE

To prevent the line of succession passing into Catholic hands and thus consolidating James II's anti-Protestant stand, in 1688 Parliament invited the Dutch ruler William of Orange to England, initially to restore lost liberties under James's rule and ultimately, if the king refused to accept the conditions laid down by Parliament, to depose James and rule in his place. William accepted, but Parliament imposed certain conditions, namely that he ruled jointly with James's eldest daughter Mary (whom William had married 12 years before) and that he accept a number of constitutional restraints on royal power. William accepted the conditions, though he had little interest in England, using this situation simply to strengthen Holland's position against France.

A RIDING ACCIDENT

William III was a slightly-built man with a passion for riding and hunting. He was an accomplished horseman, taking part in several military campaigns, and his death as a result of a riding accident in 1702 came as a great surprise.

BANK OF ENGLAND FOUNDED

The Bank of England was founded in 1694, initially to fund William's wars against France, but it later served as a means of securing government credit in peacetime. The bank moved to its present site in Threadneedle Street in 1734.

1689
Parliament issues the Declaration of Right detailing the case against James II.

1689
William of Orange is invited to rule, jointly, with his wife Mary II, James's daughter.
1689
Toleration Act allows

freedom of worship.
1689
First Mutiny Bill abolishes standing armies without permission by Parliament.

1689
Scottish-led Catholic rebellion against William crushed.
1689
Bill of Rights determines

future succession to the throne.
1689
James II defeated at Siege of Londonderry, in Ireland.

ARCHITECTURE   ARTS & LITERATURE   EXPLORATION   FAMOUS BATTLES

LOYALTY REWARDED

Henry Sidney, of Penshurst Place, in Kent was one of the leading Whigs of the day who supported James II's deposition and was one of those who invited William of Orange to take the throne. His reward was in being created Earl of Romney, as detailed in the Patent, shown left.

MUTINY BILL

One of the charges brought against James II by Parliament, which added to his unpopularity, was his raising of a massive standing army during peacetime. To prevent such a situation arising again the Mutiny Bill was passed in 1689 which forbade the raising of a standing army without parliamentary approval.

SCOTTISH REBELLION

When Charles II was restored to the throne in 1660 Scotland was once again accepted as a separate kingdom. When William III came to the throne, however, the Scots saw this independence threatened and many rebelled against his usurpation of the throne, for James II came from the royal Scottish family of Stuart. The rebellion was put down later in 1689 and the Scots made to swear an oath of allegiance to William.

GLENCOE MASSACRE

Pockets of resistance continued to exist in Scotland long after the main rebellion against William's rule was put down. A series of localised clan wars broke out, which came to a head in 1692 at the Massacre of Glencoe. Glencoe, a remote valley in the Highlands, was the family home of the Macdonalds. Under the orders of William, the rival clan of Campbell massacred many of the Macdonalds while they slept and so put down the rebellion once and for all.

WAR OF SPANISH SUCCESSION

In 1700 Charles II of Spain died without leaving an heir. The Spanish empire, which included part of the Netherlands (an area roughly corresponding to the modern state of Belgium) was settled upon Louis XIV's grandson, Duke Philip of Anjou. Louis also recognised James II's son as legitimate heir to the English throne. To prevent France from acquiring the Spanish domains, in 1701 William entered into an alliance with Holland and Austria, thus beginning the War of Spanish Succession.

✝ TOLERATION ACT

In 1689 the Toleration Act was passed which assured the freedom for all to worship as they chose, without fear of recrimination.

🔥 BATTLE OF THE BOYNE

Following James II's deposition by William of Orange, the Irish Catholics sided with James in a rebellion. The Irish Protestants, who had mostly settled around Ulster, sided with William. James first tried, unsuccessfully, to besiege Londonderry and then moved his army to the River Boyne, near Drogheda, just north of Dublin. On 1st July 1690 a pitched battle was fought, but William's superior forces quickly overran James's army, though William graciously allowed James to escape into exile, thus ending his attempt to reclaim the throne.

📜 BILL OF RIGHTS

Early in 1689 Parliament drew up the Declaration of Rights (William and Mary are shown accepting the Bill), which was afterwards consolidated as the Bill of Rights. It is usually seen as the second most important piece of constitutional legislation after the Magna Carta and reduced royal power considerably. Its most important clauses were that no Catholic could ever become the ruling monarch and taxes and laws could be implemented only with parliamentary consent.

1690	*freedom of religion in Ireland.*	**1694**	*the Electress Sophia*	**1701**
James defeated again at	**1692**	*Mary II dies; William*	*of Hanover.*	*War of Spanish*
Battle of the Boyne by	*Glencoe Massacre*	*rules alone.*	**1701**	*Succession breaks out.*
William's forces.	*ordered by William.*	**1701**	*William agrees a grand*	**1702**
1691	**1694**	*Act of Settlement settles*	*alliance between England,*	*William III dies in*
Treaty of Limerick allows	*The Bank of England founded.*	*the line of succession on*	*Holland and Austria.*	*a hunting accident.*

📖 GOVERNMENT   ⚗ HEALTH & MEDICINE   ⚖ JUSTICE   ✝ RELIGION   📜 SCIENCE

ANNE
BORN 1665 • ACCEDED 1702 • DIED 1714

nne was the second daughter of James II and Anne Hyde. She succeeded William III, her brother-in-law, in 1702, when he died without leaving an heir. She was the last Stuart monarch to rule this country. Her short reign was a strong one, bolstered by a series of military victories on the Continent, which established Britain as the most powerful country in Europe. During this period also, Parliament consolidated its constitutional successes, making the British government one of the strongest and most democratic institutions then known and the envy of other European countries.

AGE OF ELEGANCE

Anne's name was given to a period of simple, yet elegant furniture and interior decoration design, though she had nothing to do with it. Although attractive in her youth, in later years Anne herself was anything but elegant. She was grossly overweight and suffered from numerous ailments, including obesity and gout, having to be carried about in a chair. She had 18 pregnancies but all of her children died in childbirth or infancy, which probably contributed to her general ill-health.

BLENHEIM PALACE

Blenheim Palace was commissioned by Queen Anne, paid for partly by national funds, and given as a reward to John Churchill, Duke of Marlborough, in recognition of his great victories in the war with France. It was designed by John Vanbrugh and begun in 1705, though it was still incomplete when Churchill died in 1722. It now ranks as one of the most magnificent stately homes in Europe.

FIRST NEWSPAPER

Although various newsletters had been in circulation for some time, the first proper daily newspaper in London, the 'Daily Courant', was published in 1702, giving the general population access to news and events, as they happened, for the first time.

RACING AT ASCOT

Anne introduced horse racing at Ascot in 1711 thus beginning a long royal patronage that still exists today.

MONARCHY'S LAST VETO

Anne was the last monarch to veto a parliamentary bill, in 1708, when she objected to a new law to reorganise the Scottish militia. The monarchy still reserves the right of veto today, but in practice all bills receive royal approval as a matter of course.

1702 Anne, William's Sister-in-law and James II's second daughter, succeeds to the throne.	**1702** First daily newspaper in London, the Daily Courant, published. **1704** England and her allies,	under Marlborough, defeat French at Battle of Blenheim. **1704** Gibraltar taken from Spain. **1705** Barcelona captured	from Spanish. **1706** French defeated at Battle of Ramilles. **1707** Act of Union unites	the parliaments of England and Scotland. **1707** Henry Fielding, claimed to be founder of the novel form of writing, was born.

ARCHITECTURE   ARTS & LITERATURE   EXPLORATION   FAMOUS BATTLES

📜 ACT OF UNION

When James VI of Scotland was crowned as James I of England, the crowns of those two countries were united, but Scotland retained its own parliament. In 1707, however, the Act of Union was passed, uniting the governments of the two countries. The Scottish parliament was abolished, Scotland instead sending 45 members and 16 peers to the new Parliament of Great Britain in London.

◑✹ BATTLE OF BLENHEIM

Britain emerged from the War of the Spanish Succession as the greatest power in Europe, having won several notable victories under the leadership of John Churchill, Duke of Marlborough. The greatest of these was the Battle of Blenheim, fought in 1704 between the allies and the French at Blenheim, in Bavaria. The French were routed, suffering heavy losses with an estimated 26,000 dead and 15,000 captured. The War finally ended in April 1713.

📜 ACT OF SETTLEMENT

In 1701 the Act of Settlement was passed which ensured that the line of succession should pass to the Electress Sophia of Hanover, or her heirs, who were Protestants and distantly related to the Stuarts. In the event, Anne died childless and so the crown passed to James I's great-grandson, who became George I, rather than to Anne's Catholic half-brother James, the 'Old Pretender'.

📜 LAST EXECUTION FOR WITCHCRAFT

Witchcraft was still punishable by death and in 1712 the last execution of a witch took place. Practising witchcraft remained a punishable offence up until 1736 when it was abolished as a crime, in recognition that most so-called witches were not practising pagan rites but were merely local wise-women, or healers practising herbal medicine.

DUKE OF MARLBOROUGH

John Churchill was born in 1650 to a Devonshire family of quite humble status. At the age of 17 he took up military service and quickly rose to a position of distinction in the Dutch wars. At first he fought alongside James II but later changed his allegiance to William III. However, it was during the War of the Spanish Succession, between France and the allied armies of England, Holland and Austria that Churchill really came into his own, winning a series of magnificent victories that turned the tide of the war against France. He was created Duke of Marlborough in 1702.

1709
Gabriel Fahrenheit makes first alcohol thermometer.
1711
Duke of Marlborough falls into disrepute and

is dismissed from commanding the army.
1711
Queen establishes royal patronage of horse racing at Ascot.

1712
Last execution for witchcraft in England, though it is still a crime.
1712
Jonathan Swift

proposes an English Academy to 'fix' the English language.
1713
End of War of Spanish Succession.

1714
Sophia of Hanover dies, making her son George heir to the English throne.
1714
Queen Anne dies.

📜 GOVERNMENT   ⚕ HEALTH & MEDICINE   ⚖ JUSTICE   ✝ RELIGION   🜂 SCIENCE

STIRLING CASTLE

Although of much earlier foundation, the earliest part of Stirling Castle to survive dates from the 15th century, when the Stuarts converted it from a medieval fortress to a magnificent royal palace. Standing at the gateway to the Highlands, it was always considered the most vital possession during Scotland's wars of independence and changed hands more times than any other Scottish castle.

💣 BATTLE OF FLODDEN FIELD

When James IV invaded the north of England in 1513, Henry VIII sent a massive force against him. James, most of his nobility and many of the leading church dignitaries were all killed at the Battle of Flodden Field.

📖 FIRST PRINTING PRESS

The first printing press in Scotland was set up in 1507 by Andrew Myllar, under the patronage of James IV.

📖 UNIVERSITY CITIES

The early Stuart period was an age of great learning. Three universities were founded in Scotland at this time: at St. Andrews (in 1412); Glasgow (in 1450) and Aberdeen (in 1495).

JAMES I (1406-37)

James I was born in 1394 and, at the age of 12, was captured by pirates who then handed him over to Henry IV of England. Later that same year his father, Robert III, died. Despite succeeding to the throne in 1406 Henry IV held him prisoner in England for 18 years, Scotland being ruled in his absence by a regent, James's uncle, the Duke of Albany. In 1424 James was released from prison and returned to Scotland as king. During his confinement Albany had allowed many of the barons almost free rein to do as they wished and James immediately set about curbing their power. His actions won popular support, but not among the barons, who assassinated him in 1437.

JAMES III (1460-88)

When James II died unexpectedly in 1460, the throne passed to his nine year old son, James III, and Scotland was once again ruled by a regency. He assumed personal control in about 1470 but he lacked the military attributes of his father. James was a pious, well-educated man who preferred music and the arts to battle. In 1482 the border town of Berwick-upon-Tweed was lost (not for the first time) to England, but on this occasion it was to remain in English hands. James was assassinated shortly after the Battle of Sauchiebur in 1488.

Margaret of Denmark, James III's Queen.

JAMES IV (1488-1513)

James IV succeeded his father in 1488 and, like his three predecessors, was a great patron of the arts. He was also an able administrator and established Scotland as a truly united and independent nation. He built up the armed services, particularly the navy, and commissioned the 'Great Michael', which was then the largest warship in the world. In 1503 he married Margaret Tudor, Henry VII's (of England) daughter, thus briefly uniting the two countries. However, when Henry VIII invaded France in 1513 James invaded England in support of his French allies, but was killed in the process.

🏛 ARCHITECTURE   📖 ARTS & LITERATURE   ⚑ EXPLORATION   💣 FAMOUS BATTLES

THE SCOTTISH MONARCHY

THE EARLY STUARTS (1406-1513)

The Stuart dynasty, one of the most powerful royal families ever to rule Scotland, asserted their claim to power in 1371, on the death of David II. David was succeeded by Robert Stewart, his nephew, who was the High Steward of Scotland and grandson of Robert Bruce. The family later adopted the French spelling of their name, Stuart. A powerful, ambitious family, they were also great patrons of the arts and brought Scotland to the fore-front of artistic and cultural development in Europe.

JAMES II (1437-60)

James II succeeded his father in 1437 and continued the fight to quell the power of the lords, particularly in the Highlands and Isles. He fought valiantly to control the clans, particularly the Black Douglas family, who had become a law unto themselves. He finally defeated them in 1455. He was a great patron of learning and the arts and founded Glasgow University, meeting his untimely end during the siege of Roxburgh Castle in 1460 when a cannon exploded in his face.

THE ORKNEYS & SHETLANDS

Although many people regard the island groups of the Orkneys and Shetlands (right) as always having been part of Scotland, they were not in fact acquired by Scotland until 1472. Prior to that they belonged to Norway and are still proud of their strong Nordic ancestry.

LINE OF SUCCESSION

Early Stuarts (1406-1513)

James I 1406-1437
James II 1437-1460
James III 1460-1488
James IV 1488-1513

🗒 GOVERNMENT ⚗ HEALTH & MEDICINE ⚖ JUSTICE ✝ RELIGION 📕 SCIENCE

THE SCOTTISH MONARCHY
THE LATER STUARTS (1513-1625)

*T*he Stuarts were the last royal dynasty to rule an independent Scotland. James V proved a competent ruler, but the reigns of Mary and her son James VI were a sad reflection of the former greatness of earlier Stuart monarchs. The reign of James VI also witnessed the end of Scottish independence. Although a Scottish king inherited the English throne, power gradually seeped away from Edinburgh to London, until by 1707 Scotland had even lost the right to hold its own Parliament.

JOHN KNOX

John Knox was a Scottish scholar and Protestant preacher who rose to prominence in England during Henry VIII's reign. He fled to Europe in 1553 when the Catholic Mary Tudor ascended the English throne. He later returned to Scotland in 1559, assisted by Elizabeth I, and established a Protestant religion in Scotland. He died in 1572.

MARY (1542-67)
(KNOWN AS QUEEN OF SCOTS)

Mary, like so many Scottish monarchs, was a mere infant (just one week old) when she acceded to the throne in 1542. In 1548 she was packed off to France to be brought up by her mother's family, leaving Scotland once again in the care of a regency. In 1558 she married the French Dauphin and became, briefly, queen of France when he became king as Francis II, but he died in 1560 and Mary returned to Scotland the following year. She then married her cousin Henry, Lord Darnley, and became embroiled in a plot (probably against her will) to seize the throne of England.

JAMES VI (JAMES I OF ENGLAND) (1567-1625)

James VI of Scotland became James I of England when, as Elizabeth I's distant cousin and closest-living relative, he succeeded to the English throne (see pages 2-3). He had already been king of Scotland since 1567, though he was only one year old and Scotland was again ruled by a regency. Although he was himself a Protestant, he was quite tolerant of Catholics, as were other later Stuart monarchs. This led to a great deal of conflict with Parliament, who were determined to keep the monarchy Protestant.

🏛 ARCHITECTURE   📖 ARTS & LITERATURE   🏳 EXPLORATION   💣 FAMOUS BATTLES

A MURDEROUS AFFAIR

In 1566 Mary's private secretary, David Rizzio, was murdered in front of her, suspected of being her lover. She was later implicated in her husband Darnley's death and was forced to abdicate by the Scottish nobles. In 1568 she fled to England where Elizabeth I held her prisoner for 19 years before finally signing her death warrant in 1587.

FOTHERINGHAY CASTLE

It is perhaps fitting that the scene of Mary Queen of Scots' execution should itself be reduced to fragmentary remains. Fotheringhay Castle, in Northamptonshire, dates from about 1100 but was rebuilt in the 14th century. It was in the great hall, now demolished, that the pathetic figure of Mary was beheaded in 1587. Her dog is said to have crouched in the skirts of her headless corpse after the event.

JAMES V (1513-42)

James V succeeded to the throne as a 17 month old child on the death of his father at Flodden Field in 1513. Again, Scotland was ruled by a regency during James's minority, the king eventually taking full control of government in 1528. He felt betrayed by the Scottish lords and ruled very much without their consent. He proved himself to be a strong and fair king who, like his predecessors, was also a great patron of the arts.

✝ THE SCOTTISH REFORMATION

The Scottish Reformation of the church took place in the remarkably short space of 20 years, from about 1540-60. The driving force behind the movement was John Knox, a somewhat fanatical Protestant who was greatly influenced by the French theologian John Calvin. A much stricter doctrine was adopted than that followed by the Church of England, leading to the foundation of the Presbyterian Church in Scotland. In 1560 the Reformation Parliament in Scotland decided that it should be a Protestant nation.

📕 COURT OF SESSION

Despite losing its independent monarchy and Parliament, Scotland has retained its own legal, educational and religious systems to the present day. In 1532 the Court of Session was founded as the central court for civil justice.

🔥 BATTLE OF SOLWAY MOSS

In 1542 James V launched another unsuccessful invasion of England. He was defeated at the Battle of Solway Moss and died, of natural causes, a few weeks later.

LINE OF SUCCESSION

Later Stuarts (1513-1625)

James V 1513-1542
Mary 1542-1567
James VI 1567-1625
(James I of England)

📕 GOVERNMENT   🥣 HEALTH & MEDICINE   ⚖️ JUSTICE   ✝ RELIGION   📗 SCIENCE

THE STUARTS

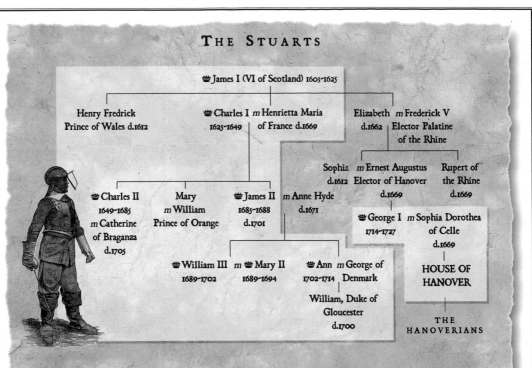

♛ James I (VI of Scotland) 1603-1625

Henry Fredrick
Prince of Wales d.1612

♛ Charles I m Henrietta Maria
1625-1649 of France d.1669

Elizabeth m Frederick V
d.1662 Elector Palatine
of the Rhine

Sophia m Ernest Augustus
d.1612 Elector of Hanover
d.1669

Rupert of
the Rhine
d.1669

♛ Charles II
1649-1685
m Catherine
of Braganza
d.1705

Mary
m William
Prince of Orange

♛ James II m Anne Hyde
1685-1688 d.1671
d.1701

♛ George I m Sophia Dorothea
1714-1727 of Celle
d.1669

♛ William III m ♛ Mary II
1689-1702 1689-1694

♛ Ann m George of
1702-1714 Denmark

William, Duke of
Gloucester
d.1700

HOUSE OF
HANOVER

THE
HANOVERIANS

The Stuarts were the ruling family of Scotland and were distantly related to the Tudors. James VI of Scotland (who became James I of England) was the great-grandson of Henry VIII's sister, Margaret Tudor, who had married James IV of Scotland. When Elizabeth died in 1603 James VI was her closest-living relative and united the crowns of England and Scotland.

ACKNOWLEDGEMENTS

This Series is dedicated to J. Allan Twiggs whose enthusiasm for British History has inspired these four books.
We would also like to thank: Graham Rich, Tracey Pennington, and Peter Done for their assistance.
ticktock Publishing Ltd., The Offices in the Square, Hadlow, Kent TN11 ODD, UK
A CIP Catalogue for this book is available from the British Library. ISBN 1 86007 020 5

Acknowledgements: Picture Credits t=top, b=bottom, c=centre, l=left, r=right, OFC=outside front cover, IFC=inside front cover, IBC=inside back cover, OBC=outside back cover.

Ancient Art & Architecture: 4 bl, 8 bl & OBC & 32tl, 9cr (Chris Hellier), 10bc, 11bc, 13tl, 16t, 17t, 28t. Archiv Fur Kunst (London): 12, 19tr, 22tl, 27t, tr & OBC. Bridgeman Art Library: 3t, 6t & OBC, 8tl, 9t & bc, 11tr & OFC, 16b, 18cl, 20bc, 21t & IFC, 31t. Mary Evans Picture Library: 2b, 3b, 4t, 6br, 6bl & OBC, 13br, 14c, 15b & OFC, 18t & b, 19cl, 21bl & OFC, 24cr, 25cr, 26cl, 28b, 29t, 30t, 31b. Chris Fairclough/Image Select: 5t, 9cl, 17cl, 21cr. Hulton Getty Collection: 22cl, 23t. National Maritime Museum (London): 14b, 15t, 23bl, 30b. National Portrait Gallery (London): 7r & OFC, 10tl, 13tr, 14t, 19tr, 26tl. Ann Ronan/Image Select: 22tr. Spectrum Colour Library: 24bl, 29b

Every effort has been made to trace the copyright holders and we apologise in advance for any unintentional omissions.
We would be pleased to insert the appropriate acknowledgement in any subsequent edition of this publication.

Printed in Italy

A 1,000 YEARS OF BRITISH HISTORY - THE MILLENNIUM SERIES

BOOK I (1,000~1399)   BOOK II (1399~1603)   BOOK III (1603~1714)   BOOK IV (1714~ present day)